ROBOTS

DON'T HAVE TASTEBUDS

BY TIM RADES

ISBN-13: 978-1-7349552-0-0

To my Big Guy, Jagger

SO YOU'D LIKE TO BE A ROBOT

MADE OF METAL, WIRES AND SCREWS.

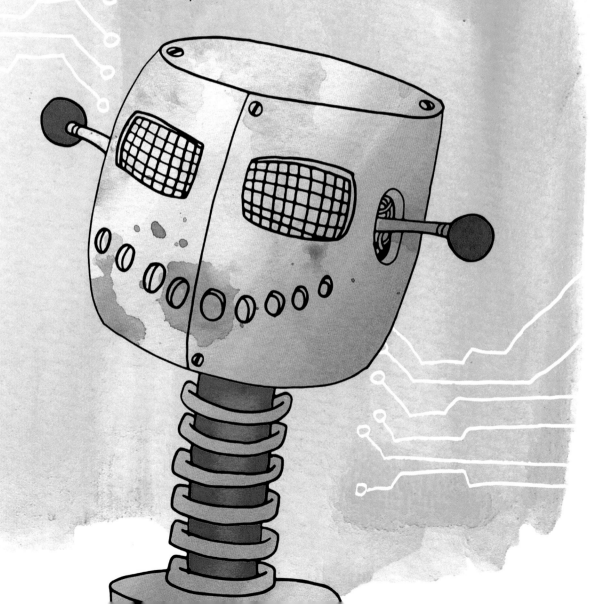

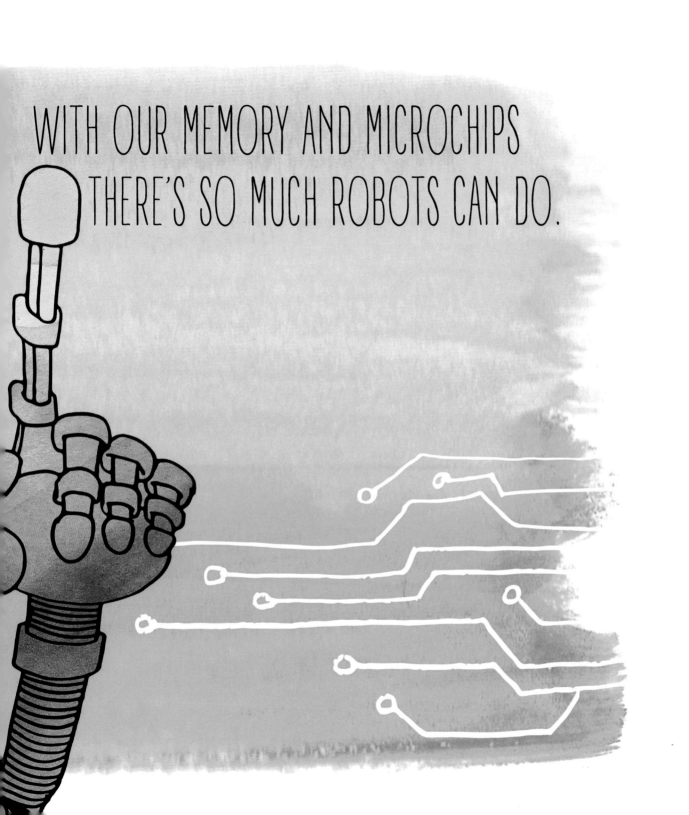

WITH OUR MEMORY AND MICROCHIPS
THERE'S SO MUCH ROBOTS CAN DO.

WE HAVE SUPER SIGHT THAT CAN SEE FOR MILES

AND WE CAN ALSO SEE THROUGH WALLS.

OUR ROBOT LEGS ARE ADJUSTABLE.

WE CAN BE SHORT
OR WE CAN BE TALL.

OUR HYPER SPEED CAN TAKE US

HERE TO THERE IN NO TIME FLAT.

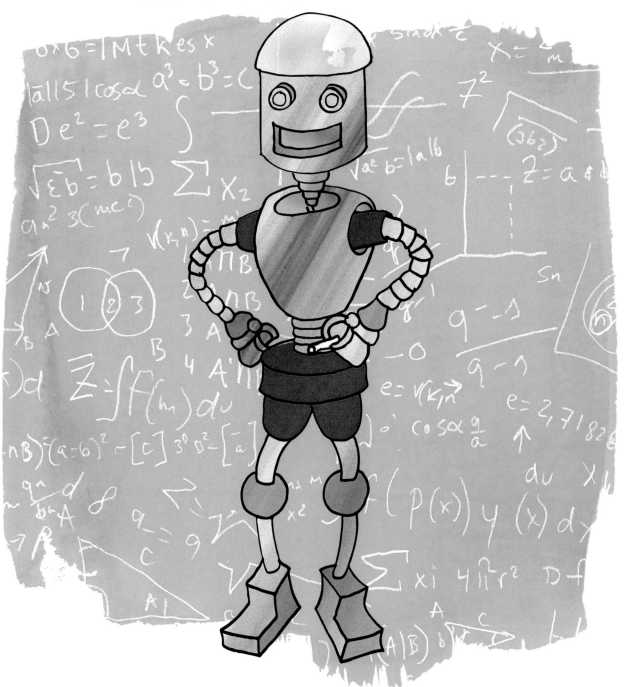

WE CAN ALWAYS TAKE THE HEAT

AND WE CAN ALSO TAKE THE FROZEN.

WE CAN ALWAYS GET A QUICK REPAIR

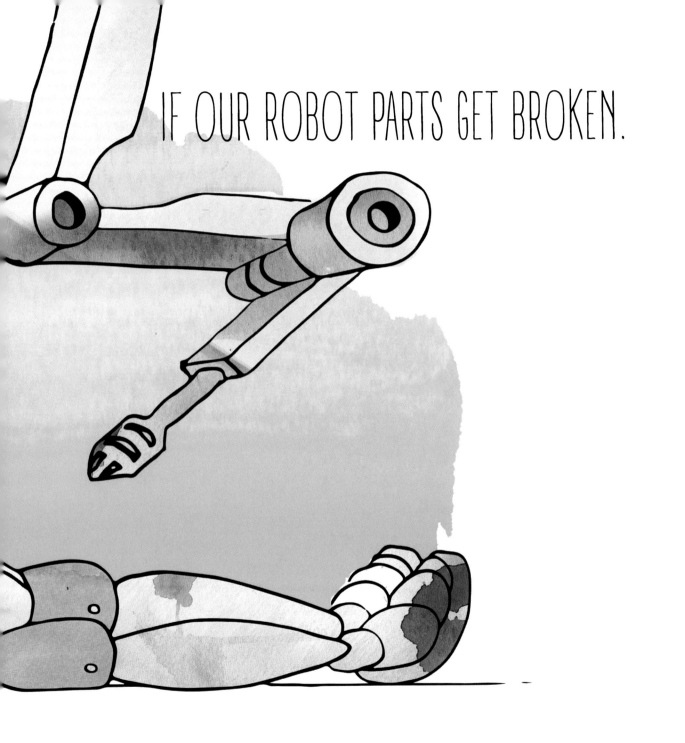

IF OUR ROBOT PARTS GET BROKEN.

SOME ROBOTS ARE FOR CLEANING

AND SOME CAN EVEN FLY.

BUT
THERE'S ONE THING
THAT BUMS
ROBOTS OUT

AND I'M HERE TO TELL YOU WHY.

ROBOTS

DON'T HAVE TASTEBUDS

AND THAT MIGHT NOT SOUND LIKE MUCH,

IT'S REALLY PRETTY TOUGH.

WE CAN'T TASTE COTTON CANDY

OR BIRTHDAY CAKE ICE CREAM,

OR CANDY CORN FROM HALLOWEEN,

OR CRISP TORTILLA CHIPS,

THE SAVORY SALT OF PISTACHIOS

OR (QUESTIONABLE) BLACK LICORICE,

THE OOEY GOO OF PUDDING

OR JIGGLY GELATIN THAT'S HOMEMADE,

THE FIZZINESS OF A ROOTBEER FLOAT

THE CRUNCH OF CELERY AND CARROTS

OR MASHED POTATO SPUDS.

THESE ARE THE THINGS WE MISS THE MOST 'CAUSE WE DON'T HAVE TASTEBUDS.

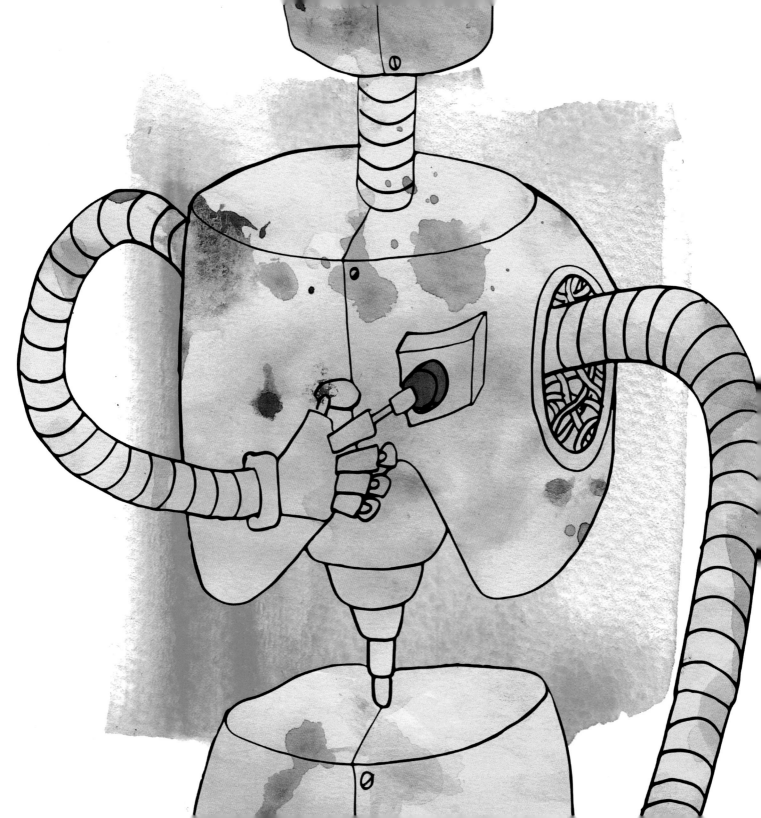

WE
ONLY HAVE A
BUTTON
THAT YOU PRESS
ON
TO START

BUT YOU CAN APPRECIATE THE TASTE OF THINGS,

Made in the USA
Las Vegas, NV
31 August 2021